D0118950

To my mom, with utmost love and gratitude
—M. C.

To our final jewel, Baby Jane, who is beautiful and dimpled
—A. H.

SIMON & SCHUSTER BOOKS FOR YOUNG READERS

An imprint of Simon & Schuster Children's Publishing Division

1230 Avenue of the Americas, New York, New York 10020

Text copyright © 2008 by Mary Casanova

Illustrations copyright © 2008 by Ard Hoyt

All rights reserved, including the right of reproduction in whole

or in part in any form.

SIMON & SCHUSTER BOOKS FOR YOUNG READERS is a trademark

of Simon & Schuster, Inc.

Book design by Jessica Sonkin

The text for this book is set in Venetian.

The illustrations for this book are rendered in pen and ink

with watercolor on Arches paper.

Manufactured in China · 10 9 8 7 6 5 4 3 2 1

Library of Congress Cataloging-in-Publication Data

Casanova, Mary. · Utterly otterly day / by Mary Casanova ;

illustrated by Ard Hoyt.— · 1st ed. · p. cm.

Summary: After a day out on his own, Little Otter realizes that

he still needs his family no matter how big he grows.

ISBN-13: 978-1-4169-0868-5 (hardcover)

ISBN-10: 1-4169-0868-4 (hardcover)

[1. Otters—Fiction.] I. Hoyt, Ard, ill. II. Title.

PZ7.C266Ut 2008 · [E]—dc22 · 2007041428

BY Mary Casanova

Utterly Otterly Day

PICTURES BY
Ard Hoyt

SIMON & SCHUSTER BOOKS FO   New York · London · Toronto · Sydney

Little Otter wakes in his safe, snug den,
ready to play
in an utterly otterly way.
He tugs Sister's whiskers,
wrestles Mama's tail,

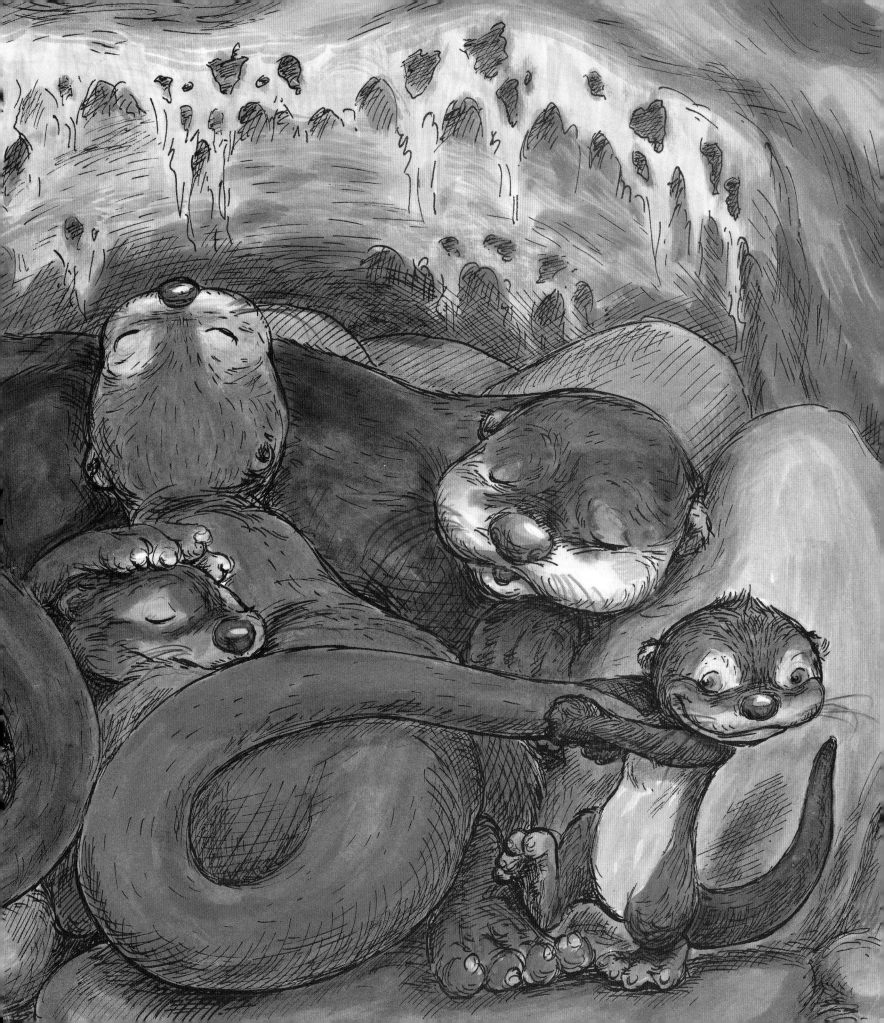

then slides out the tunnel—

whippidy, slippidy, sail!

"Stay close," whuffs Papa.
"Be careful," Mama chirps.
But Little Otter bounds away—
he's a big otter now—
he knows not to stray.

Little Otter cracks clams.

Clickety, clunkety, crunch!

He floats with schools
of slick silver fish.

Milky, silky, swish!

"Be careful, be careful," seagulls screech.
He's a big otter now—

he twirls away—
just out of Eagle's reach!

He bobs up near Beaver,
who chews and chomps,
in her bobbily beaverly way.

"Watch out," she warns.

Whappity, slappity, SMACK!

He's a big otter now—

creak,
crack,
WHACK!

Little Otter dives deep.
Dizzily, whizzily down!

He bumps into Turtle's toes,
jaggedy shell, and sharp snapper nose.

He's a big otter now—
he swerves—

and speeds away.

Soon his tummy rumbles—grumbles!
Time for something to munch.
Snacks from a bucket, better eat fast.
Fisherman's coming . . .
free minnows won't last!

He hides by pelicans,
who slurp up fish
in their perfectly pelicanly way.

Swishily, swashily, swish!

Mama and Papa suddenly pop!
"Little Otter," they chirp,
"sun's sinking low. . . ."
But Little Otter wanders away—
he's a big otter now—
still time to play!

Up a steep slope he climbs.
His family circles below.
"Little Otter," they huff and whuff,
"Little Otter—time to go!"
Little Otter leaps toward the top,
higher and higher . . .
then skids to a

STOP!

Ravens quit cawing.
The forest grows still.
Something stirs
beyond the hill.

Now Cougar's eyes narrow.
Her belly sweeps low.
She quietly, cunningly creeps.
She slinks and she sneaks.
She waits . . . and waits . . .

Mama and Papa screech and cry,
"Look out, Little Otter!
Danger nearby!"

Cougar pounces,
all claws and snarls!
Cougar snaps,
all teeth and growls!

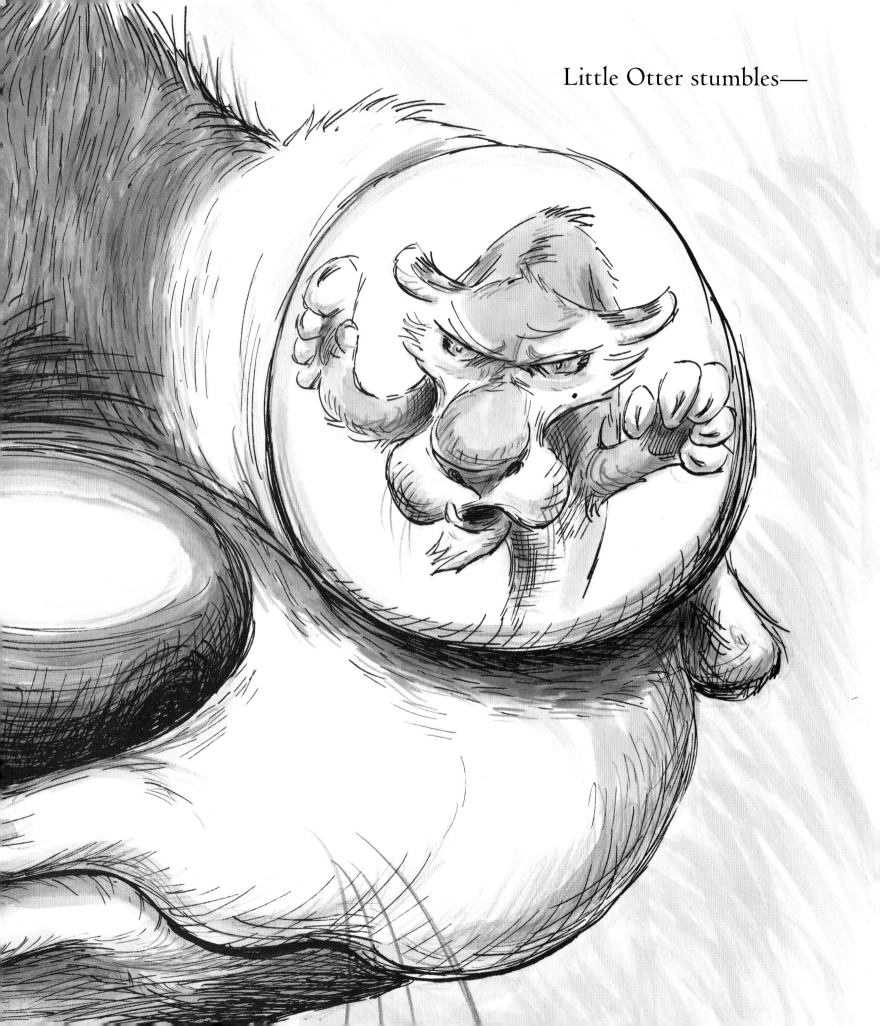

Little Otter stumbles—

Then lickety-split,
he twists and turns!
He flops and flips!
He gives a screech—

somersaulting out of reach!

Slip! Slide!

Down the hill,
the otters dart and swoosh.

Then—whooooosh!

They hide inside their den.

Little Otter shakes and shivers.
Little Otter quakes and quivers.
Papa snuggles, nuzzles. . . .
Mama tenderly preens,
until—lick by lick—
Little Otter is clean.

His paws stop trembling.
He tucks tail to nose.
He needs his family—
no matter *how* big he grows.

Then Little Otter closes his eyes
and dreams in a sleepy otter way
of his whippidy, slippidy,
swishily, swashily,
dizzily, whizzily,
warily, scarily . . .

utterly otterly day.